AF484612

J.C. HULSEY BOOKS

THE LAST RIDE

A WESTERN SHORT

J.C. HULSEY

For information contact: jchulsey1@att.net
Cover Coloring & Design by J.C. Hulsey
Published by J.C. Hulsey Books
September 2020
10 9 8 7 6 5 4 3 2 1

CHAPTER ONE

I had been riding for four days straight, without stopping and I was give out. I only stopped to relieve myself and give Horse a little water.

Horace Gilderslaw had killed Old Man Grisham and fled on a stolen horse.

The town council wanted to form a posse to go after Gilderslaw, but since I'm the sheriff of Bluebell, Texas, it was my call and I convinced them it would take too long to round up a posse and I could make better time traveling alone.

They agreed, which wouldn't have mattered to me whether they agreed or not, I usually did things my way. After collecting a few provisions on a pack mule and saddling Horse, I set off to bring back this killer.

~~~~~~~~~~~~~~~~

On the morning of the fourth day, after passing through a small town called Hadlie's Crossing, we reached the small deserted town of Hendersonville, a
~~~~~~~~~~~~~~~~

small mining town that went belly up when the mines gave out. A chilling wind blew around the corner of the buildings bringing with it a passel of weeds and dust. I reached back, untied my poncho and slid it over my head. I could already fill the warmth seeping into my bones. I positioned it so my pistol was clear. There had been more than one person that lost his life because they couldn't get to their weapon. That wasn't gonna happen to me. I gave Horse his head and rode straight down Main Street. As I rode, I constantly scanned the alleys and roof tops for any sign of movement.

One man with a rifle hiding on top of one of these buildings could take me out easily, providing he was a good shot. If there was an easier way to flush him out, I sure didn't know it. I thought I saw movement, so I pulled up on the reins and slid to the ground. I took cover beside some crates in the closest alley. I scanned the street, the buildings and then I spotted him. He was squatted down behind the facade on the deserted bank building. I walked backwards into the alley behind the building. I worked my way down until I could cross the street without being seen. I went behind the row of buildings until I reached the bank. I flattened myself against the wall next to the rear door, reached slowly and tried the knob. It twisted and opened. I carefully opened it just wide enough to slip through. I walked softly to the bottom of the stairs.

'Wonder if he's still up there? If he's not, I could be in a heap of trouble. He could be hiding anyplace. Well, I won't find out standing here.'

I placed my foot on the first step. It creaked and groaned with my weight. I froze and held my breath. I was sure he could hear my heart beating because I sure could. In a few seconds when nothing happened, I began the ascent up the stairs, stopping on each step to listen.

I held my gun ready in case he had heard the creaking stairs. When I reached the top step, I hesitated again. Squinting into the simi-dark space ahead, I thought I saw movement, but couldn't be sure. I stood plastered to the wall, hoping, if it was him, that he couldn't see me. Apparently, he didn't, because he walked down the hallway away from me. He reached the last door and went in. Stepping away from my hiding place, I carefully walked in his direction. I had just reached the door, he had gone into, when it opened and I found myself face to face with him. I was extremely lucky for he had his pistol in its holster. I poked him in the gut with the barrel of my weapon and heard a loud whoosh as the breath left his body. He stumbled back into the room sprawling onto the floor. I quickly stepped inside and covered him with my gun.

"I've got you now. As soon as you catch your breath, sit up."

He wheezed and coughed, then sat up. "You didn't have to do that. You could've broke a rib or something."

"I don't want to hear no bellyaching from you. You're lucky I didn't shoot you. That's what you deserve, after what you did."

"That was an accident. I was only gonna rob that old man, but then he fought back and I hit him. He should have done like he was told."

"Well, he didn't do what he was told and you killed him. Don't make no never mind that you didn't mean to, you did and now you gotta pay."

"I reckon they're gonna hang me, ain't they?"

"You'll get a fair trial. But yeah, they'll probably hang you. Old man Grisham was very well liked in Bluebell. You better hope and pray they don't lynch you before you get that trial. You feel like getting up?"

"I don't suppose I could talk you into letting me go?"

"Not a chance. Come on, let's go. It's a long ride back to town."

He stood slowly, bent at the waist, holding his belly. All of a sudden, he stood up straight and grabbed my gun hand. He was extremely strong for such a small man. We wrestled and he caught the pinky figure of my hand and twisted. I had to turn loose of the gun. It splattered to the floor and was kicked to the side as we continued to scuffle. As I said he was strong and my entire hand was throbbing where he had twisted my finger. We wrestled on the dusty floor with him on top. He got in a couple of licks that stunned me. But I twisted him over where I was on top. I was getting tied. If I was, surely he was too. I landed a haymaker alongside his head that put him out of commission.

I sat up and leaned back against the wall, taking deep breaths. Maybe I'm getting too old to be wrestling with somebody. Or maybe it's sitting behind that desk all day. Well, better do this. It ain't gonna do itself.

I slowly got to my feet, walked to where my gun was, bent and picked it up, then slid it in the holster. Next, I picked up my hat, slapped it against my leg and put it on. Gilderslaw was moaning and turning over. I said to him, "Alright, you ready now to head back to town or are we gonna have to tussle again.

He sat up, rubbing his jaw where I had clobbered him. "You hit pretty hard for an old man."

"Unless you want me to hit you again, I would recommend you settle down and let's head to town."

"Okay," he said as he stood, retrieving his hat on the way. "I know when I'm licked."

"Hold out your hands," I ordered.

"Why?" he whined. "You ain't gonna cuff me, are you?"

"That's just what I'm gonna do. I figure if you're cuffed, you might not try nothing. Where's your horse," I asked.

"He's in the livery stable, where would you put your horse?"

"Okay, let's go," I nodded toward the open door.

He started walking and when he reached the door, I said, "Hold it a minute." I reached and picked up his six shooter and stuck it in my waistband. "Okay, go ahead, and remember I got you covered."

I followed him as we left the building and headed down the street to the livery stable.

"You do realize," he started speaking. "My brothers ain't gonna let me hang."

"I don't reckon they're gonna have any say in it. It's gonna be a jury of townsfolk that decide whether you hang or not."

"You must not have heard me," he fussed. "I said my brothers ain't gonna let me hang. Don't make no never mind what no jury says. They won't let nobody put no noose around my neck."

"Let me tell you so's you understand," I said quite loudly. "I'm the sheriff of Bluebell, have been for a few years now. If your brothers come to town and cause trouble, then they'll probably be on the scaffold beside you. Now that's something you can believe."

We reached the livery and walked inside. There was one horse.

"I can't saddle my horse with these hand cuffs on."

"That's okay, I know how to saddle a horse. You move over to that stall over on the other side while I do it."

I got the saddle and bridle on his horse and started leading him outside.

"You gonna let me mount up or you gonna make me walk all the way to town?"

"You can mount up when we get my horse. Ain't gonna have you ride off without me."

"You sure are cautious ain't you?"

"This ain't my first rodeo," I answered.

Horse was standing where I had left him, munching grass as if everything was right in the world.

I mounted up, then handed the reins of his horse to Gilderslaw. "Okay, you can mount up now."

He climbed into the saddle fussing because he had hand cuffs on. "This would be a whole lot easier without these irons."

"You'll survive. Now head out," I ordered.

After four days in the saddle, then wrestling with Gilderslaw, I was beginning to feel effects of the trip without having any rest. Maybe it would be best to stop for an early camp and I could get a couple hours sleep. Just enough to rejuvenate this old body.

"Pull into that little grove up ahead. We'll camp there for the night."

"You think that's a good idea? I'm a desperate criminal. I might knock you in the head and ride on outta here."

"If you can ride handcuffed to a tree, then have at it."

"You ain't gonna cuff me to no tree are you? It ain't human."

"Dismount and gather some firewood, stay so's I can see you."

He climbed off his horse and began gathering sticks and limbs for a fire.

"Build it and light it," I told him. I was really beginning to give out. *'Maybe I should cuff him to the tree before I pass out.'* "That's enough wood. Come on over here and sit by this tree."

"If I promise I won't run, will you leave me loose?"

"Sit down," I ordered. He sat and I released one cuff. "Now," I said. "Hug the tree."

I fastened the cuff to his wrist and stood. Walking to my horse, I untied my bedroll, spread it beside the unmade fire, laid down and was asleep before I closed my eyes.

CHAPTER TWO

"Hey! HEY! Wake up!" I heard a voice, but it didn't register with my tired brain. "HEYYY! WAKE UP!"

My eyes fluttered open. Immediately, I was on my feet, my gun in my hand, wondering where I was. Recollection came slower than usual. I really need to think about turning in this badge.

"Great! You're awake, finally. You need to take these cuffs off or else I'm gonna be needing a new pair of pants."

I walked slowly to him. "I orta leave you to do your business right where you're at, it's what a low down skunk like you deserves, but I am, after all, a human being that's gonna grant your wish."

"Thank you kind sir," he said sarcastically.

"Be nice. I ain't took them off yet." I removed the cuff from his left hand. "I'm gonna watch you, so do what you got to do at the edge of the camp. Don't go no further, 'cause I will shoot you."

He walked to the edge of the camp, took care of his business and walked back.

"How about you building a fire and we can have some bacon and beans."

"Ain't it supposed to be the other way around? Ain't the sheriff supposed to feed the prisoner?"

"I can always let you hug the tree while I build the fire and cook a meal. It's your choice."

"Okay, I understand. How about taking this other cuff off? It's bothersome swinging loose like this."

"I reckon you'll adjust to it soon enough."

He had a small fire going in a short time.

"Stuff's on the mule. And while you're at it, unsaddle the horses and bring the saddles over here. Make a pot of coffee first."

He did as he was told, although I could hear him muttering about it. He carried both saddles and set them down, then walked back to the mule and took out a can of beans and a small slab of bacon from the pack. He carried them to the fire, set them down and went back for a skillet, plates, cups and a couple of spoons. He pulled out a coffee pot and brought everything back to the fire.

He had coffee going in no time. He poured a cup and began walking toward me.

"Hold on," I warned. "Just hand it slow and easy."

I took the cup and waited until he turned back to the fire before I blew on the hot liquid, then sipped it slowly. It sure hit the spot.

"How am I supposed to cut this bacon and open these beans?"

"There's a knife and a new-fangled thing called a can opener in the pack. Remember, I'm watching everything you do."

I pulled the brim of my hat down and squinted into the fading yellow sun as it began its descent behind the horizon. I had a feeling it was gonna be a long night. Maybe we should ride through the night. That way we wouldn't have to ride facing the morning sun.

CHAPTER THREE

The bacon was sure smelling good. "How about it? Is it 'bout ready?"

"Yeah, I reckon it's as good as it's gonna get. You gonna dish it up for yourself or do I bring it to you?"

"I 'spose I can get it myself. You go ahead and get yours, then go back to your tree."

I watched while he filled his plate and walked back to the tree, then I stood and filled a plate for myself.

If we didn't get on the road soon, that sun would be beating down on us most of the day. I sure wasn't looking forward to it because I already had a blinding headache.

"Alright, pack up everything and let's get on the road."

"You ain't gonna help?"

"You're a grown man. I don't figure you need no help. Now, get a move on. I'm gonna saddle my horse." I stood and walked to Horse. He was happy that I was finally paying attention to him. I scratched between his eyes and he murmured to let me know he liked it.

I began saddling him when I heard graveling crunching close behind me. I whirled around and found Gilderslaw holding the skillet in the air, fixing to take a swing at me.

I ducked as fast as I could and deflected it with my arm. It hurt like hell fire, but I countered with a fist to his midsection.

He grunted, dropping the cast iron skillet and doubled over grabbing his stomach.

I hit him again and he slumped to the ground. "When you gonna learn?" I growled at him. "You enjoy pain, is that it?"

He rolled over on his side, looked up at me with tears in his eyes. "Can't you hit a feller anyplace besides his gut? I think you might've broke a rib."

"Let me explain the rules to you. Maybe you forgot who the prisoner is here and who is in charge. I'm in charge and you're the one going back to town to stand trial. Now, there's one more thing you need to know and you had better listen and learn. You better burn it into your thick skull. You try anything else, if you just blink your eyes the wrong way and I'm gonna put a slug in that gut of yours. Shake your head if I'm coming through to you and you understand."

He nodded his head that he understood. I stuck my hand out and he grabbed it as I began to pull. He stood slowly still holding his gut.

"Finish packing up," I told him. "Then saddle up and let's get out of here."

We were still standing very close when I heard the shot as it whizzed by my ear and Gilderslaw cried out and fell into me. I grabbed him and let him slip to the ground. The side of his head was bleeding and his breathing shallow. I quickly moved away as another shot kicked up dirt as I dashed behind a tree.

The shots continued slamming into the tree. I glanced over at Gilderslaw and he wasn't moving. The only ones I could think off that might be following was his brothers.

"Hey! Out there!" I shouted. "I'm the sheriff of Bluebell. I'm taking a prisoner back to stand trial. Your bullet hit him and he needs to be looked at. If he dies, I'll be arresting you for his death."

More shots slammed into the tree, then stopped.

"You! Sheriff! You say Horace is shot?"

"Yeah! Your first shot got him and it looks bad. Maybe you should ride for the doctor while I look at him."

"We're putting down our guns and coming out! Don't shoot!"

I peeked around the tree and saw two hombres stand up with their guns holstered and step out toward the injured prisoner.

"Horace!" one of the men yelled and rushed over, knelt down and cradled the man's head in his lap. "Horace! Oh my God, what have I done? I done killed my little brother."

I stepped from behind the tree with my .45 trained on the two men. "Your names Gilderslaw?" I asked.

The one still standing nodded and said, "Yeah. We're the Gilderslaw brothers and Horace is our baby brother."

"How bad is he?" I asked the one holding Horace.

"He's still breathing, I think," he answered. "I shore didn't mean to shoot him."

"Don't matter whether you meant to or not. You did. Now one of you needs to ride for the doctor while I see what I can do to save your brother. There's a small town just south of here a couple of miles."

"I'll go," the older brother said, and hurried off.

"What's your name?" I asked the other brother.

"Hank," he told me. "You gonna help Horace?"

"I'm gonna try. You move outta the way and shuck you gun while you're at it. I don't need to be watching you while I look at Horace."

"I ain't gonna shoot you, cause you're helping my brother," he removed his gun and tossed it aside.

"Go add some wood to the fire and heat some water. There's some whisky on the pack mule. Get it and get a clean shirt too."

Horace was breathing but it didn't look good. His skin color was washed out and his breathing labored. There wasn't a lot of blood which wasn't unusual for a head wound. Hank came back carrying a bottle of whisky and a couple of shirts.

I tore a strip from the shirt and poured some whisky on it. I wiped and dabbed it against the wound. I could see the white skull where the skin was opened with an inch-wide gash.

"Hank, get some blankets!" Horace was beginning to shiver. Even unconscious, shock was beginning to set in. I had seen a lot of injuries like this. Some made it, some didn't, so I figured Horace had a fifty-fifty chance. I covered him with the blankets Hank brought over.

"That's all I can do for him now. Best thing is to keep him warm. Why don't you grab the coffee pot and make some coffee? Looks like we ain't going no place anytime soon."

It wasn't long until Hank and I were sipping hot coffee.

"Hank, how old are you?" I asked.

"I'm twenty-seven. Why?"

"I figured you and your brothers was a lot younger."

"Why'd you figure that?"

"These stupid stunts you keep boys pulling. It's things a bunch of young kids would do."

"You don't understand about us. We had a hard upbringing. Our pa and ma mistreated us something awful."

"Maybe so, but the way I figure is you can't blame your ma and pa for the things you done after you left home. Way I see it is you're responsible for your own deeds. It's about time you boys grew up."

"When's Harry getting back?" Ignoring what I said. He shoulda been back before now."

"It's a two hour ride there and a two hour ride back, so it's gonna be a while yet. Throw another log on the fire and relax. Tell me more about your childhood?"

"Ain't nothing else to tell. Our folks were about the meanest folks around and they beat us every time we blinked."

"You sure you're not exaggerating?"

"Exger . . . what?"

"Exaggerating. It means you ain't telling the truth. You sure you boys didn't do something to deserve a spanking?"

"Weren't no spanking?" he moaned. "They beat and whipped us with most anything they laid their hands on. Down-right mean, I tell you."

"Even so, you should still take responsibility for your actions. Can't blame your folks for things you do now."

"I don't wanta talk about it no more. You gonna take Horace to jail, that is if he wakes up?"

"Yeah, I reckon that's what I'll do because he killed a man and he has to pay."

"I didn't know he killed no body. You figure he'll hang?"

"Ain't for me to decide that. That's up to a jury. He'll get a fair trial."

What about me and Harry? We shot at you and hit Horace. You gonna arrest us and put us in jail?

"What do you think I should do?"

"I don't rightly know. You could let us go. After all, we was just trying to help our baby brother."

"Now, you think on that for a minute. Did you break the law when you and your brother shot at me, me being the law? Did your brother Horace break the law when he took another man's life?'

"I reckon since you put it that'a way. Yeah, we all done broke the law."

"What happens to lawbreakers? Or a better question is, what do you think should happen to lawbreakers?"

"I don't rightly know, especially since it's me and my brothers. Maybe if it was somebody else I could give you an answer, but I just can't, being it's us."

"What made you come after Horace and willing to shoot and maybe kill the one who held him prisoner?"

"Why, that's easy. He's our baby brother and I reckon that's the reason. He's our kin and we love him."

"This man in Bluebell that Horace killed. You think maybe his kin might feel the same way about him? You think his wife, his kids or his brothers might feel the same about him?"

"I think I see what you mean."

"Let's say if I did let you go, I would be breaking the law that I've sworn to uphold. If no one upheld the law, then what kind of country would we have? Would you want to live and raise your kids where there is no law?"

CHAPTER FOUR

"Huum," Mumbling came from Horace. Hank jumped up and rushed to his side. "Horace, it's me. Hank. Can you hear me, Horace?"

"He's still out of it. He was just mumbling in his sleep. But it's a good sign, him mumbling. Means he's still alive. A lot of folks injured like him ain't lasted this long."

"So you think he's gonna be okay?"

"We'll know more when the doctor gets here."

"Look, there comes Harry and the doctor. I sure hope he's a doctor."

The two men stopped their horses and dismounted. The man in the black suit untied a black bag from the saddle horn and hurried over to Horace.

"He looked at him, then turned and said, "Get me some hot water and be quick about it."

"Get it, Hank," I told him, while watching Harry. I had a feeling he was going to be trouble. Why don't you come over here and sit down," I said to him, rather loudly.

He turned from watching the doctor and looked squarely at me. "I'd rather stand where I'm at, if that's alright with you, Sheriff?"

"Well, it ain't alright with me. I'm telling you to shuck your gun and come over here and sit down."

I could see his mind churning trying to figure if it was worth it or not. He finally shrugged his shoulders, came over and sat down.

"You forgot something," I sat as he sat on a rock next to the fire.

"What are you talking about? I came over to the fire like you told me."

"You forgot your gun," I said, nodding the gun on his hip.

"I didn't forget my gun. It's right here," he reached for his gun. But, before he cleared leather, my slug knocked him onto his back.

"What did you do that for?" he shouted, as blood leaked through his fingers where he was holding his arm. "I was just taking my gun out like you asked! You didn't have to shoot me."

"You should have told me what you were doing, then you wouldn't be laying on the ground with a slug in your shoulder. Doc, you better take a look at him before he loses too much blood."

"He'll be okay until I finish here. Did you shoot this one too?" he asked.

"Nope, it was these two brothers of his."

"Brothers?" he exclaimed. "Was they mad at each other?"

"They was shooting at me and missed. How's the patient?"

"He's got a fair chance. If he lasts a few more hours, he should be fine. Now, let me look at your shoulder," as he stood and walked to his new patient.

"Ow!" Harry shouted. "Take it easy!"

"Don't be such a baby," the doctor said. "Let me take a look or not. It's up to you." He started to stand.

"Okay, okay, please do something. It burns like the fires of hell."

The doctor ripped his shirt and probed for the bullet. Harry was doing a lot of loud moaning and gritting his teeth. He didn't, however, say anything to the doctor as he pulled out the slug and dropped it in the fire.

"There you go," said the doctor. "Good as new, almost, as he wrapped a bandage around Harry's arm and rigged a sling for it. "Got any more victims I should look at, Sheriff?" he asked sarcastically.

"I reckon you fixed them all up," I fired back just as sarcastically. "I appreciate you coming out," I told him, a little easier.

"No problem," he replied. "That's what I signed up for. Although when I got my medical degree, I sure didn't figure on digging bullets out would be the main thing I do."

"You gonna head back to town or you gonna go back with us, that is if Horace gets well enough to travel."

"I'll stay until he wakes up or not, that is until morning, then I've got to go check on Mrs. Freeman. She's due anytime and although she's done this eleven times, I feel I need to be there just in case."

"Hank," I said loudly. "Make a fresh pot of coffee."

"Yes sir," Hank jumped as if something had kicked him in the butt. "You want me to cook some beans too?"

I looked at the doctor who shrugged his shoulders. "Sure," I said. "Fix a proper meal. Beans, taters and bacon."

"Sure thing Sheriff." Hank began stirring the coals, bringing the fire to life.

CHAPTER FIVE

"That was good," the doctor said as he rubbed his stomach.

Just then, Horace moaned and started to sit up. The doctor jumped up and rushed to him. "Easy fellow, don't try to sit up," as he gently pushed him back onto the pallet.

"Where am I?" Horace asked, barely audible.

"You've been shot, but you're gonna be alright, if you just lie still and rest."

"Who are you and where am I?" Horace asked again.

"I'm Doctor Nelson and you've been shot. Now rest easy and you're gonna be fine."

Horace seemed to relax, closed his eyes and lay still.

"Doctor Nelson pulled the blanket up around his neck, stood, looked at me and the boys and said, "He's gonna be okay. I wouldn't move him yet, but he's gonna be okay. I reckon I better move out and check on Mrs. Freeman."

"How soon can he fork a horse?' I asked.

I don't think he should be moved for a couple days, at least. Of course, if you had a wagon, I reckon it'd be okay."

How much I owe you?" I asked.

"I figure five dollars should cover it. Is that agreeable with you, Sheriff?"

"It's agreeable if you can wait till I get back to town. I don't have five dollars on me. I'll send it to you."

"I reckon if you don't have it, I'll call it even for the meal. If you're ever in Sosolita, you can bring it by my office. So long." He headed to his horse, mounted up and took off to the south.

CHAPTER SIX

"Harry, you feel up to going to look for a wagon?"

"What are you talking about? Did you forget I got a hole in my arm, which you put there?"

"I didn't forget, but I reckon you ain't hurt enough that you can't ride, that is if you want to help your baby brother."

"What's Horace got to do with this?"

"Didn't you hear the doctor? Said he couldn't ride for a couple of days. We ain't got enough grub to last that long."

"I sure don't feel like riding on a wild goose chase, hunting no wagon. My arm hurts like blue blazes."

"I know what we can do," said Hank. "We can rig a travois. Indians use them all the time. Should work as good as a wagon."

"I ain't riding on no travois," exclaimed Harry.

"It ain't for you, Hank. It's for Horace. Why you being such a pain?"

"You're lucky I'm hurt or I'd show you what pain is."

"Okay, Hank," I said. "You figure you can fix up one of them travois?"

"Sure, Sheriff, I reckon so. You willing to let me have my gun back in case I run into a snake or some kind of varmint?"

I tossed his pistol to him. "Just remember, I'm no varmint," I told him.

He caught his gun, holstered it and headed through the brush.

I stood, walked over to Horace, knelt down and felt his forehead. It was cool to the touch and his breathing sounded normal. I stood, walked to the fire and poured a cup of coffee.

"What's you gonna do with us when we get back to town?" Harry asked.

"First, I'm gonna lock you in a cell, then I'm gonna get me some rest."

"You just gonna go off and forget about us?"

"No, I ain't gonna forget about you. It's just that I need to get caught up on my rest. This has been one long tedious ride."

"What you gonna do if we decide not to go back with you?"

"Let me tell you how it's gonna be. You remember how that slug in your arm burned? I believe you said it burned like the fires of hell. You remember?"

"Yeah, I remember, so?"

"It'd hurt a lot worse if that slug was in your gut. So I'd recommend you not even think about not going back with me."

Hank came through the brush carrying an arm load of long poles. "I think I can make these work," he said excitedly. He laid them out in a row, walked to his horse, removed his rope and came back. "I could use a little help," he said looking at his brother.

"I'm hurt," Harry said a little too loud.

"Harry," said Hank. "You may be the oldest, but right now you're acting like a baby. You ain't hurt so bad that you can't lend a hand so's we can get our brother to town."

"Why do we want to do that? They're just gonna hang him and us along with him. No sir, I ain't anxious to get hanged."

"They ain't gonna hang us, are they Sheriff?"

"I can't answer that truthfully. But if Horace didn't mean to kill Old Man Grisham, the jury might let him off easy. As for you two, I don't reckon I'll prefer charges against you, since you're both being so helpful." I looked at Harry.

"Okay. Alright. I hear you. I'll help build the travois."

CHAPTER SEVEN

We got Horace loaded onto the travois without much trouble. He was still drifting in and out of consciousness, murmuring a few words as he did so.

"Alright fellows," I stated. "Let's mount up and move out. Hank, you watch your brother close. Let me know if it looks to be too rough for him."

"I'll do that Sheriff. I'll watch real close."

"Why don't we ride to Sosolita?" Harry asked. "It's only a couple hours to the South."

"'Cause I ain't the sheriff there and the murder happened in Bluebell."

"You really think Horace killed somebody?" Hank asked.

"He told me he did, although he did say it was an accident."

"You reckon the jury will take that into account?"

"That's something I can't answer," I replied.

We turned our horses into the sun and headed out. I had an uneasy feeling that this was going to be a long, long ride.

CHAPTER EIGHT

We had to travel slow because of Horace, and let me tell you, I was feeling as if I had been dragged by a team of horses. I could feel myself drifting off more than once.

"Sheriff?" It was Hank. "Sheriff?" he spoke again.

"Yeah," I answered.

"You okay. I mean you look like you're fixing to fall outta the saddle."

"I'm okay," I said, even as I felt my body go limp and I slid to the ground, as the blackness closed in on me.

"Sheriff," I heard a voice in the murky darkness. "Sheriff!" It was a little louder this time and I felt something cool on my face.

"Where am I? What's going on?" My brain was all fuzzy.

"It's alright. I'm Hank Gilderslaw. This is my brother Harry and that one on the travois is my baby brother Horace. You're the sheriff and you's taking us back to Bluebell. Don't you remember?"

My brain felt like a bowl of mush. The thoughts were rushing through my head it seemed like ninety miles an hour. They were rushing so fast I couldn't grab onto one enough to remember.

"I figure since he don't know nothing or remember nothing, we orta take Horace and ride on outta here," I heard one of the men say.

"We can't do that," I heard the other man say.

"Sure we can. He ain't nothing but a broke down old man laying flat of his back. Did you forget he's taking us back to stand trial, maybe to hang?"

"Water? Water?" I heard a feeble voice asking for water, then I realized it was my voice.

"He's burning up with fever. Get the bedrolls. We need to keep him covered. Make him sweat. Get plenty of liquid in him."

"I say let's leave him here and ride on out."

"Harry," I heard the younger voice. "Have you always been so mean? I can remember when you cared about things. I remember when you found that rabbit with the broken leg. You carried that rabbit home and nursed it till its leg was healed. What happened to you?"

"That rabbit weren't taking me back to jail or maybe worse."

"Well, you can ride out if'n you're amind to, but I'm staying."

I felt that cool feeling on my face again. "Let me hold you up so's you can take a bit of water." I felt or at least I thought I felt a hand behind my head lifting me up and then I felt cool liquid against my lips. I opened my mouth and the liquid passed over my lips and down my throat. Then the darkness came again.

<div align="center">~~~~~~~~~~~~~~~~~</div>

I could feel the sweat running down my spine as I faced the gunman. He had only been in town for an hour and already three men were lying in the street. His name was Bart Hunsaker. Hunsaker was known throughout the territory as, Black Bart, the cold-bloodied killer. He killed for no known reason. Some said he laughed as his victims lay bleeding on the ground. A merciless laugh that sounded inhuman.

I stood facing him now and for the first time since I pinned on this badge, I was feeling fear. A cold deadly fear that today I would be leaving this world, and I wasn't ready. I had too much living left to do.

What happened next is unexplainable. At least I couldn't begin to explain or even understand.

I watched as Hunsaker drew his gun before my hand had even touched the handle of mine. It seemed time slowed to a crawl and I watched as a trickle of sweat slowly rolled down his face. I watched as he pulled back the hammer on his .45. I watched as he squeezed the trigger and then nothing. No, I don't mean nothing that way. I was still standing. I was still alive. His .45 hadn't fired. I drew my weapon and fired. My shot was true. Hunsaker folded and fell to the ground. His face had a look of astonishment as he fell face down into the dirt.

~~~~~~~~~~~~~~~~

I could hear voices again. This time they seemed closer. I opened my eyes slowly. I saw a bright yellow moon in a purple sky. I tried to sit up, but quickly fell back to the pallet.
~~~~~~~~~~~~~~~~

"Hey, Sheriff," I heard a familiar voice. "It's good to see you getting better. You've had a rough time of it. Here, let me help you up for a swig of water."

The liquid was so much better than the last time.

"How long we been here?" I asked with a voice I didn't recognize.

"Three days," he answered. "I'm sure glad you're alright. Harry, bring some of that soup over here for the sheriff. It's rabbit soup. Harry went hunting and came back with a couple of rabbits. We roasted them for ourselves, but saved some to make this soup for you and Horace."

"Horace? He okay?"

"Yep, he's just about ready to get off that travois and ride a horse. Just as soon as you're up to it, we'll be ready to move out. Here, take some of this soup," he held a spoon in front of my mouth.

When I swallowed, that soup really hit the spot. That empty spot down in my belly. I could feel the energy as it spread through my body. When the cup was empty, I couldn't hold my eyes open any longer. I lay back and was instantly asleep.

This time the dreams were better. There I was, standing behind a tree on the bank of the little creek, watching as Marylou Banister was swimming. She hadn't seen me and if I had my way, she wasn't going to see me. A more beautiful sight I had never seen in all my born days.

"Are you gonna stay behind that tree or are you gonna join me?" Marylou's voice jerked me out of my dreamlike trance. I stepped from my hiding place, my face as red as a beet.

"Well," she said, a little louder. "You gonna join me or not?"

Being a sixteen-year boy, I stood there, my body paralyzed. I couldn't make my legs work. The heat from my face began to creep down my whole body. I closed my eyes, swallowed the lump in my throat, then opened my eyes to see Marylou, stand up in the shallow water, and began to walk toward me.

~~~~~~~~~~~~~~~~
~~~~~~~~~~~~~~~~

"Sheriff. Sheriff!" I heard that familiar voice and felt something pushing on my shoulder. "Time to wake up and eat something. You ain't gonna get no better if'n you don't eat."

I struggled to sit up and even though it was hard, I managed. I glanced around the camp and spotted Harry and Horace talking over by the horses. Hank was by the fire filling a tin plate with what looked like beans. He carried it back and handed it to me.

"You gonna be able to fork them beans or you want me to spoon feed you like I did the soup?"

"I reckon I'll be able to get'em down. Thanks."

Them beans and bacon was about the best meal I ever had and in no time at all the plate was empty.

"Here's some coffee to wash it down," Hank handed me a steaming cup of black liquid.

I took it, feeling the heat through the side. I raised it to my lips, blew on it, then took a small sip. Just like the beans and bacon this black liquid was filled with energy that I knew I needed.

"How come you boys stuck around?" I asked Hank.

"Now Sheriff," he said. "We ain't bad people. We couldn't just ride off when you was feeling poorly, now could we?"

"I'm obliged to you," I told him. "I figure a couple hours and I'll be ready to ride."

"If'n you think you'll be ready, we'll be ready."

I lay back and closed my eyes. I was definitely feeling a lot better, with a full belly and rid of the fever. I don't know how long I slept, but I was awakened by voices. Loud voices.

"I don't care!" I recognized the voice. It was Harry. "I stayed till he got over the fever. Now me and Horace are gonna light outta here.

I raised my head as best I could and saw the three brothers standing by their saddled horses. It looked like Harry was set on riding out, even if he had to leave his brothers behind.

"Harry, I just don't understand why you want to run out on us. I thought you cared about us."

"I do care, but I care about my neck just a little more. You know he's taking us back to stand trial and there ain't no telling what a judge and jury will do. I ain't willing to take that chance."

"You heard the sheriff say he wasn't gonna press charges against us if we helped him. You heard him same as I did."

"Yeah, I heard him, but he's the law. He might change his mind when we get back. He done told me first thing he's gonna do is lock us up.'

"How do you feel about it Horace? After all you're in more trouble than we are."

"I reckon I'm willing to take my changes 'cause the sheriff saved my life. That's what you told me. I did kill that old man, even though I didn't mean to."

I reached around searching for my pistol and found it laying by my bedroll. I grabbed it as I sat up. Cocking it, I shouted, "I done told you what would happen if you tried to escape. You do remember, don't you Harry?"

It looked like Harry was gonna go for his gun when Horace put his hand over his brother's hand.

Harry looked at his brother, then at me. He must have figgered it was more trouble than he was willing to get into. He raised his hands in mock surrender. "Okay. okay, I won't cause no more trouble."

"That's a very good choice," I said as I eased the hammer of my gun down. "Now, let's see if we can get packed up and on the move before the sun gets too high in the sky."

I rolled over and struggled to my feet. Me being sick had taken a lot out of me, but I'm a stubborn old cuss and I made it to my feet, although my head began throbbing something awful. I squinted my eyes against the pain and placed my hat gently on my head.

The brothers worked pretty well together, braking camp and in a short while Hank declared, "We're ready when you are Sheriff."

"Alright, mount up and head out."

CHAPTER NINE

I was struggling to get up and into the saddle when Hank rode up. "Let me help," he said as he jumped off his horse and pushed me into the saddle.

"Thanks," I mumbled, feeling a little ashamed of them seeing me in this condition.

Even worn out as I felt, it did feel good sitting in the saddle, where a good cowboy needs to be.

"You don't got to worry none Sheriff," Hank said. "We ain't gonna cause no trouble. We'll accept whatever the judge and jury decides is right. We all agreed."

"I'm sure glad to hear that, 'cause I kinda like you boys. Wouldn't wanta shoot none of you."

"You know what Sheriff?" Hank asked.

"What?"

"We don't want you to shoot us neither." He kneed his horse and caught up with his brothers.

Even though Hank had told me they didn't want no trouble, I had a little niggling feeling between my shoulder blades that Harry wasn't sold on the idea. He kept looking back at me and touching the handle of his gun each time.

I sure hoped he didn't try nothing 'cause the way I was feeling, I don't think I could get my gun out and fire before he got me.

"Hold up, fellows!" I yelled.

They pulled up and stopped each turning their horse toward me. "What is it Sheriff?" Hank asked.

"I'd feel a whole lot better if you boys would hand over your six guns."

"Why? What did we do wrong?" asked Hank.

"You didn't do nothing wrong. It's just I'd feel better holding on to your guns."

"Sure, Sheriff, I understand." Hank rode up close and gave his pistol to me.

"I don't have one," said Horace. "Remember you took mine way back when we first met."

"Sure, I remember. What about you Harry?" I asked as I placed my hand on my weapon.

I thought for a minute there he was gonna challenge me, but he rode up close and handed his weapon over.

"Thanks fellows. I feel much better now."

They turned their horses back down the trail with me following behind.

It was an uneventful ride until the sun began disappearing behind the horizon.

"Hold up fellows," I called to them. We need to look for a place to make camp.

"I'll scout ahead and find a place," Harry said loudly and took off up the trail."

I was slow in reacting and he was out of sight before I realized he was gone.

"Don't worry Sheriff," Hank said. "He'll be back." His voice didn't sound very convincing.

"That looks like a good spot up there in those thickets. Let's camp there. I'm plumb tuckered out."

"I'll gather firewood," Horace said.

"I'll take care of the animals," Hank said. "You just rest easy Sheriff. We'll have some coffee in a bit. Sit over by that tree and rest."

"I sure appreciate you boys being so co-operative."

"Shucks, it's like I told you before. We ain't real bad people. It's just sometimes we make wrong decisions."

"We all make wrong decisions. It's what we do when we make wrong decisions, is what counts and you boys are taking care of that, at least two of you are."

"Harry will come back. I know he will. He's just a little confused, that's all. He'll be back."

"I hope so, 'cause it'll be better for him if he does."

Horace came back with the firewood and starting building a fire. Hank began unsaddling the horses. I sat down and leaned back against a tree. The next thing I knew was someone pushing on my shoulder.

"Sheriff. Sheriff, you okay?" It was Hank.

I opened my eyes and saw his face. "Are you okay?" he asked again.

I reached my hand up and wiped my face, all of a sudden remembering where I was. I knew right then, at that moment, when I got back to Bluebell, I was gonna turn in this blasted badge.

"Sure Hank, I'm okay. Reckon I'm still feeling a little tired. That's all. Something sure smells good."

"Yeah, there's coffee and what's left of the beans and bacon. You sit still and I'll fetch you some."

He hurried back to the fire and started dishing up a plate full. Horace poured a cup of coffee and handed it to his brother.

"Here you go Sheriff," he handed me the cup. "It's real hot."

"Thanks Hank," I said. "You're a good kid." I blew into the cup a few times, then carefully sipped the black liquid."

"I'll set the plate right here next to you," he said.

I had just reached for the plate when a shot rang out and the plate jumped into the air as the slug hit it. I only thought I was feeling bad and not able to move, because when I heard that shot, I was behind the tree in no time flat, with my pistol in my hand. I peeked around edge of the tree and didn't immediately see anybody, but then off to my right I saw him, it was Harry. I hated to kill him, but it might be necessary if I couldn't talk him out of killing me.

"You okay, Sheriff?" Hank asked from his hiding place.

"I'm okay. How about you and Horace?"

"We're both fine. You know who's doing the shooting, I reckon."

"Yes. I know and it ain't looking good for him. You think you can talk some sense into him?"

"I'll sure try. Harry! This is Hank, what are you doing? You know you're only making it worse. Stop shooting and let's go back to town with the sheriff."

"I ain't going to jail. I'd rather be dead."

"If you don't stop shooting, you won't have to worry about going to jail. You're headed for the grave yard. Now throw out your gun and let's head to town."

He answered with another slug bouncing off the tree I was behind.

"Harry, this is your little brother Horace and I'm asking, no I'm begging, please don't do this. I'm the only one in trouble here. At least I was the only one in trouble. Maybe if you give up, the sheriff will go easy on you."

"Listen to Horace, Harry. He's telling you the way it is. Give up. The sheriff's a fair man. Come on. Give up."

"You need to listen to your brothers Harry. I will either take you back one of two different ways. One being riding upright in the saddle or thrown across it. It's your choice. What's it gonna be?"

Another slug bounced off my hiding place.

"Well, I reckon I got your answer." I peeked around and let off two shots in his direction, hoping I wouldn't hit him. I sure wasn't in the mood to kill nobody and surely not a kid like Harry, but sometimes moods change and mine was right on the verge.

"Harry," I called. "How about if I told you, that you wouldn't spend any time in jail? Would you be willing to talk about it?"

No answer, which I could interpret he was at least thinking about it. Then another shot.

"Dang fool kid." I peeked around again and shot twice, this time aiming to hit him.

"Ugg." I heard him yell. My shots must have been true.

"Harry! You alright?" Yelled Hank and then Horace. "Harry! Answer us. Please answer us."

Harry didn't answer.

"Lord let him just be hurt and not dead," I prayed. I stood and walked to where he was lying, face down and not moving. I knelt beside him and felt for a pulse. Nothing. *'What have I done? You didn't have a choice. He gave you no choice.'*

Horace and Hank rushed up and stopped, looking at their brother lying in the dirt.

"Is he . . . is he dead?" Horace asked, his voice quivering.

I stood. "Looks like it. You both realize he gave me no choice."

"We ain't blaming you Sheriff. We heard you try to talk him out of it. We just wish you hadn't killed him."

"I'm sorry, boys, but like I said, there was no other way. He made his choice."

"I reckon he got what he wanted," Horace said.

"How's that?" I asked.

"He said he'd rather be dead than go to jail. I reckon he got what he wanted." Horace said as a tear rolled down his cheek.

"Can we bury him here Sheriff?" Hank asked, "We don't want nobody to see him like this."

"Sure that'd be okay 'cept for one thing."

"What?" Hank asked.

"We ain't got no shovel."

"That's okay, we can dig a shallow grave with a flat stick or something."

"Go ahead, but be as quick as you can. We need to get on the road. It's still a long ride back."

The boys made short time of burying their older brother and we were back in the saddle and on our way.

CHAPTER TEN

We rode into town late stopping in front of the jail. I was still feeling poorly and not in a very good mood. I think having to kill Harry was a little too much for me. Oh, I've killed many men in my life as a lawman, but maybe it's 'cause I'm getting old, this one really got to me.

"You boys take the horse to the livery and come on back to the jail."

"You're trusting us to not run away?" Hank asked.

"I ain't worried. I think you boys will do the right thing. Now go on and get the horses stabled. Tell you what. Instead of coming back to the jail, come on down to the café. I could use a good meal right about now."

"Sure Sheriff, come on Horace." They took the reins of my horse and headed for the livery stable.

I stepped up on the boardwalk feeling an ache in my legs and back. Maybe a good steak will make me feel better. I reached the café and opened the door. The room was empty except for Amber and Andrew Sloggins, the owners.

"Howdy Bart," said Andrew. "You okay. You look a little pale. Did you catch Gilderslaw?"

"Howdy Andrew. Miss Amber. Yeah, I caught him and his brothers. And yes, I'm feeling a little poorly. I thought maybe a good meal would perk me up."

"Steak and potatoes okay?" asked Amber as she headed for the kitchen.

"Wouldn't want nothing different. Cook up a couple more. The Gilderslaw brothers are coming behind me."

"You didn't lock them up?" asked Andrew.

"No. There're a couple of pretty good boys. They helped me when I needed help. I trust them completely."

"You said a couple which implies two. I thought there was three brothers."

"There was. Had to kill the oldest. He didn't want to go to jail. Got some coffee?"

"Sure, I'll get some." He stood and headed to the kitchen. He was back almost immediately with a pot and four cups. "If you don't mind, I'll join you with a cup."

"Don't mind at all. I always enjoy visiting with you."

The bell over the door rang as the door opened and Hank and Horace came in. They walked over to the table and stood with their hats in their hands.

"Okay. Sit yourself down. I ordered for you. Have some coffee until the meal's ready."

They sat down with their heads bowed, not wanted to face Andrew.

"Sheriff tells me you boys helped him quite a bit."

"Weren't nothing," said Hank. "The sheriff is a mighty fine man. We was glad to help."

Amber brought out three plates loaded with steak and gravy, potatoes and a large helping of green peas. I could feel the strength coming back into my body just by looking at the meal.

"Come on Andy. I'm sure the sheriff wants to talk to the boys."

Andrew stood and walked away with his wife, disappearing into the kitchen, leaving me alone with the brothers.

"Dig in boys. This could very well be the last good meal you will enjoy for quite a while. Pour me another cup of coffee, will you?"

Hank poured the coffee and asked, "You think the Judge will hang us?"

"No. I think Horace might have to serve some time, but after I talk to him, maybe he'll go light on him. As for you, what do you recommend I do with you?"

"I reckon if somebody took a shot at me, I'd lock him up for quite a spell."

"The Judge would probably agree with you, if I didn't say nothing, but I plan on saying my piece."

"What are you gonna say?"

"First of all, it's what I ain't gonna say that's important. I ain't gonna say nothing about you shooting at me. But I am gonna tell how you and Horace took care of me when I was sick and you didn't run off like you could have. I'm gonna tell how I think both of you boys need another chance. I'm, also, gonna tell him that I'm willing to hire you on at my ranch, when I retire. I'm gonna tell him I'll be responsible for the two of you, so if he lets you go with me, I'm gonna expect you to stay outta trouble."

"Are you gonna retire? You really giving up your badge?"

"Yep. Out on the trail I decided this was my last job. I'm getting too blasted old to be shooting at folks and getting shot at. I'm turning it in first thing tomorrow. Now finish up, 'cause you're gonna have to stay in jail until the Circuit Judge comes to town."

"When will he be here?"

"Let's see. What's the date today? I reckon he should show up in a couple days. In the meantime, let's go."

EPILOGUE

It's been two months since I turned in my badge. The Mayor and the town council tried to talk me out of it, but I told them I'd had enough. I was gonna raise horses from now on out. The boys stood trail and the Judge said because I stood up for them, he would let them come home with me. He finished it up with, if either one of you so much as look the wrong direction, the jail is always here.

They've been a couple of good hands. Hank has been talking about going to school to be a veterinarian. Horace is the quitter of the brothers and says he is happy staying here taking care of the horses.

There is another reason I'm enjoying not being Sheriff. Widow Hansan is the dressmaker in town. She has always showed a bit of interested in me, but she made it very plain that as long as I was Sheriff, she wouldn't or couldn't get involved with me. Some folks might say, why should she be able to dictate what you do for a living. Well, I reckon a woman has a hard enough time without having to wonder if her man is gonna come back or not, so yes, I'm enjoying retirement and very thankful this was my **Last Ride**.

Other Titles by J.C. HULSEY

Angel Falls, Texas

Velvet Sky, Arizona

Angry Orchard, Colorado

Clear Stone, Wyoming

Itching Tree, Idaho

Windy Butte, New Mexico

Devil's Dance, Dakota Territory

Redemption Road

Red Rose

Rebecca

The Concho Kid

Ugly Mugly

GUTSHOT

The Last Ride

The Old Man

The Pistol Preacher

Shortland

Dynamite

The Concho Kid

Dead Man's Gun

Does Nora Know

Doke Walker

Brothers

Satan's Refuge

Shadrack

The Brute

The Decision

The Greenhorn

The Gunfight

The Hangman

The Old Timer

Trudy

Ugly Mugly

The Waterhole

Welcome to Texas Hell

Some Stuff I Wrote

Some More Stuff I Wrote

Even More Stuff I Wrote

Newest Stuff I Wrote

Brand New Stuff I Wrote

Brand Spanking New Stuff I Wrote

Look What I Found

Oldest Coon Hunter in Somervell Co

(Compiled by)

Confessions of a Battered Wife

(Compiled by)